Geronimo Stilton
ENGLISH!

16 LET'S GO TO THE FARM! 到農場去！

新雅文化事業有限公司
www.sunya.com.hk

Geronimo Stilton English
LET'S GO TO THE FARM! 到農場去！

作　　者：Geronimo Stilton 謝利連摩・史提頓
譯　　者：申倩
責任編輯：王燕參
封面繪圖：Giuseppe Facciotto
插圖繪畫：Claudio Cernuschi, Andrea Denegri, Daria Cerchi
內文設計：Angela Ficarelli, Raffaella Picozzi
出　　版：新雅文化事業有限公司
　　　　　香港筲箕灣耀興道3號東匯廣場9樓
　　　　　營銷部電話：（852）2562 0161
　　　　　客戶服務部電話：（852）2976 6559
　　　　　傳真：（852）2597 4003
　　　　　網址：http://www.sunya.com.hk
　　　　　電郵：marketing@sunya.com.hk
發　　行：香港聯合書刊物流有限公司
　　　　　香港新界大埔汀麗路36號中華商務印刷大廈3字樓
　　　　　電話：（852）2150 2100　　傳真：（852）2407 3062
　　　　　電郵：info@suplogistics.com.hk
印　　刷：C & C Offset Printing Co.,Ltd
　　　　　香港新界大埔汀麗路36號
版　　次：二〇一二年一月初版
　　　　　10 9 8 7 6 5 4 3 2 1

ISBN: 978-962-08-5491-0
© 2008 Edizioni Piemme S.p.A., Via Tiziano 32 - 20145 Milano - Italia
International Rights © 2007 Atlantyca S.p.A. - via Leopardi, 8, Milano - Italy
© 2012 for this Work in Traditional Chinese language, Sun Ya Publications (HK) Ltd.
9/F, Eastern Central Plaza, 3 Yiu Hing Rd, Shau Kei Wan, Hong Kong
Published and printed in Hong Kong

CONTENTS
目錄

BENJAMIN'S CLASSMATES

班哲文的老師和同學們

Maestra Topitilla
托比蒂拉・德・托比莉斯

Rarin
拉琳

Diego
迪哥

Rupa
露芭

Tui
杜爾

David
大衞

Sakura
櫻花

Mohamed
穆哈麥德

Tian Kai
田凱

Oliver
奧利佛

Milenko
米蘭哥

Trippo
特里普

Carmen
卡敏

Atina
阿提娜

Esmeralda
愛絲梅拉達

Pandora
潘朵拉

Takeshi
北野

Kuti
菊花

Benjamin
班哲文

Hsing
阿星

Laura
羅拉

Kiku
奇哥

Antonia
安東妮婭

Liza
麗莎

GERONIMO AND HIS FRIENDS
謝利連摩和他的家鼠朋友們

謝利連摩·史提頓 Geronimo Stilton
一個古怪的傢伙，簡直可以說是一隻笨拙的文化鼠。他是
《鼠民公報》的總裁，正花盡心思改變報紙業的歷史。

菲·史提頓 Tea Stilton
謝利連摩的妹妹，她是《鼠民公報》的特派記者，同
時也是一個運動愛好者。

班哲文·史提頓 Benjamin Stilton
謝利連摩的小侄兒，常被叔叔稱作「我的
小乳酪」，是一隻感情豐富的小老鼠。

潘朵拉·華之鼠 Pandora Woz
柏蒂·活力鼠的姨甥女、班哲文最好的朋友，
是一隻活潑開朗的小老鼠。

柏蒂·活力鼠 Patty Spring
美麗迷人的電視新聞工作者，致力於她熱愛的電視事業。

賴皮 Trappola
謝利連摩的表弟，非常喜歡食物，風趣幽默，是一隻饞
嘴、愛開玩笑的老鼠，善於將歡樂傳遞給每一隻鼠。

麗萍姑媽 Zia Lippa
謝利連摩的姑媽，對鼠十分友善，又和藹可親，只想將
最好的給身邊的鼠。

艾拿 Iena
謝利連摩的好朋友，充滿活力，熱愛各項運動，他希望
能把對運動的熱誠傳給謝利連摩。

史奎克·愛管閒事鼠 Ficcanaso Squitt
謝利連摩的好朋友，是一個非常有頭腦的私家
偵探，總是穿着一件黃色的乾濕褸。

跟我謝利連摩·史提頓一起學英文，就像玩遊戲一樣簡單好玩！

你可以一邊看着圖畫一邊讀。
以下有幾個標誌，你要特別留意：

當看到 🔘 標誌時，你可以聽CD，一邊聽，一邊跟着朗讀，還可以跟着一起唱歌。

當看到 ⭐ 標誌時，你可以和朋友們一起玩遊戲，或者嘗試回答問題。題目很簡單，它們對鞏固你所學過的內容很有幫助。

當看到 ❗ 標誌時，你要注意看一下格子裏的生字，反覆唸幾遍，掌握發音。

最後，不要忘記完成小測驗和練習冊裏的問題！看看你有多聰明吧。

祝大家學得開開心心！

謝利連摩·史提頓

親愛的小朋友，你喜歡農場生活嗎？我是一隻非常喜歡住在城市的老鼠，但我也喜歡到住在農莊的羅莎婆婆家去，我還會幫忙照顧農莊裏的動物和果樹呢！我以一千塊莫澤雷勒乳酪發誓，成熟的士多啤梨和剛從樹上摘下來的蘋果的香氣是多麼吸引啊！我已經等不及要和菲、班哲文和潘朵拉一同出發，開始一段美妙的農莊之旅了！

GRANDMA ROSA'S FARM
羅莎婆婆的農場

我們剛剛抵達羅莎婆婆的農場，羅莎婆婆已在門口迎接我們了。這是潘朵拉第一次去農場，於是羅莎婆婆向她介紹農場裏的每個地方。

weather vane

farmhouse

hay

greenhouse

straw

porch

hayloft

well

courtyard

cowshed

vegetable
garden

1 Here is our house! The bedrooms are upstairs.

2 The fields are behind the house.

3 The orchard is down there.

4 May we go up there in the hayloft, Uncle Geronimo?

field

orchard

5 Uhm... of course, but later!

rabbit warren

hen house

feedstuff

sheep fold

6 Let's go to the cowshed first. Come on Pandora!

9

FARM ANIMALS
農場裏的動物

我以一千塊莫澤雷勒乳酪發誓，農場裏的動物真多啊！而且牠們每一隻都非常可愛，潘朵拉看得眼花繚亂，她沒法決定自己最喜歡哪一隻。

cow

horse

sheep

bull

rabbit

pig

goat

donkey

lamb

calf

dog

cat

A SONG FOR YOU!

Track 1

This Little Cow

This little cow eats grass
this little cow eats hay
this little cow drinks water
this little cow runs away
this little cow does nothing
but lies down all day.

Give her, give her, give her a flower!
Give her, all give her, give her a flower!

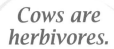
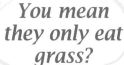

A Rhyme

There's a cow in
the cowshed,
there's a cow in
the cowshed,
there are a cow
and a calf
in the cowshed.

There's a sheep in
the sheep fold,
there's a sheep in
the sheep fold,
there are a sheep
and a lamb
in the sheep fold.

⭐ 試着用英語説出下面的
動物名稱：綿羊、豬、
驢子。

POULTRY 家禽

多新鮮的雞蛋啊⋯⋯羅莎婆婆每天都從雞棚中撿出新鮮的雞蛋。
班哲文和潘朵拉也想幫忙撿雞蛋，希望他們能小心點，可別把雞蛋打碎了。

cock
hen
chick
goose
duck
turkey
pigeon
turtle-dove
peacock

> goose　鵝
> geese（goose的眾數）鵝

Look! There are some turtle-doves next to the hens!

The cock is crowing at the top of its voice!

Hens lay eggs!

The chicks scratch about: they are so sweet!

Geese honk!

The peacock spreads its tail!

The countryside is beautiful... but I miss home!

THE TRACTOR　拖拉機

我想嘗試駕駛拖拉機，而班哲文和潘朵拉則想去餵動物們吃東西。羅莎婆婆和羅德公公很高興有機會教小孩子們一些新東西。

what 什麼

They eat fresh grass, or hay.

What do cows eat?

Hay is grass which has been cut and dried in the sun.

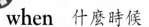

when 什麼時候

The grass is tall! When are you going to cut it?

Tomorrow! Then we let it dry.

Dried grass will turn into hay!

Where is the hay stored?

In the hayloft!

where 哪裏

To feed the farm animals in winter.

Why is the grass left to dry?

why 為什麼

IN THE VEGETABLE GARDEN
在菜田裏

在羅莎婆婆的農場裏還種了有機蔬菜和水果。班哲文和潘朵拉正在學習怎樣用英語說出每種蔬菜的名稱。你也跟着一起學習吧!

POTTERING IN THE VEGETABLE GARDEN
在菜田裏耕種

能幫羅莎婆婆幹一些農活真好！在農場裏要做的事情真多呢，要是能有多幾隻手爪就好了。

Benjamin picks strawberries.

Tea picks apples from the apple tree and puts them into a basket.

Rododendro makes holes in the ground with a hoe, to plant tomatoes.

In the middle of each hole, Pandora puts a small tomato plant.

Grandma Rosa shells the peas and puts them on a plate.

Geronimo waters the salad plants.

Let's Go Together to the Farm!

I sow the corn and what about you?
I pick apples and what about you?
I milk the cow and what about you?
I groom the horse
and what about you?

Grandma Rosa has a farm,
a beautiful, beautiful,
beautiful farm!

I plant beans and what about you?
I pick apricots and what about you?
I give grass to the rabbits
and what about you?
I sow potatoes and what about you?

I pick salad and what about you?
I plant tomatoes and what about you?
I water strawberries
and what about you?
I give corn to the hens and what about you?

Grandma Rosa has a farm,
a beautiful, beautiful,
beautiful farm!

Grandma Rosa has a farm,
a beautiful, beautiful, beautiful farm!

Grandma Rosa has a farm,
a beautiful, beautiful,
beautiful farm!

〈農場神秘事件〉
羅莎婆婆的農場位於瑪思卡波湖附近。
謝利連摩：我們來了，羅莎婆婆。
羅莎婆婆：謝謝你們，謝利連摩！快，牠們都走了出來。

羅莎婆婆：那些母牛整個星期都是這個樣子，牠們沒有生產牛奶了。

史奎克：牠們好像很傷心。

羅莎婆婆：究竟發生了什麼事？

史奎克：最近有沒有不尋常的事情發生過？

羅莎婆婆：嗯……我種了一些番茄。

羅莎婆婆：這會有影響嗎？

史奎克：每一個細節都是破案的關鍵！

史奎克：天色越來越暗了，我們回去睡覺吧！

Night falls on the farm. Everybody is sleeping.

ZZZ ZZZZ

But a good detective...

... keeps watch even in his sleep!

CRACK

Just as I thought!

在農場裏，現在已經是深夜了，大家都在睡覺。
但是有一個精明的偵探……
卻假裝在睡覺，其實正窺探着四周的動靜。

史奎克：果然不出我所料！

Case solved very easily!

史奎克：事情很快就可以解決了。

Turn around slowly...

...Grandma Rosa?!?

史奎克：慢慢轉過身來……

史奎克：羅莎婆婆？！？

就在這個時候，謝利連摩被嘈吵的聲音弄醒了，他也來到屋外。

謝利連摩：這麼晚了，你們在這裏做什麼？

羅莎婆婆：我在跟植物聊天，希望它們能快高長大！

羅莎婆婆：我每晚都會來給番茄講故事。

史奎克：現在我明白了！

史奎克：那些母牛是妒忌，因為沒有鼠給牠們講故事……

謝利連摩：所以牠們很傷心。

羅莎婆婆：好……我知道該怎樣做了。

於是……

羅莎婆婆：……從此以後，他們便快樂地生活在一起了。

史奎克：事情終於解決了。

謝利連摩：恭喜你……但是請幫幫我吧！

TEST 小測驗

⭐1. 用英語説出下面的詞彙。

> **(a)** 田地　**(b)** 菜田　**(c)** 果園　**(d)** 乾草　**(e)** 温室　**(f)** 庭院

⭐2. 用英語説出下面的句子。

(a)
> 菜田在那兒下面。
> **The ... ... is ... .**

(b)
> 我們可以上去那兒嗎？
> **May we ... ... ?**

(c)
> 誰吃粟米？
> **... eats corn?**

(d)
> 母牛吃什麼？
> **... do ... eat?**

⭐3. 你知道下面的動物用英語怎麼説嗎？試説説看。

(a) 母牛　**(b)** 公牛　**(c)** 兔子　**(d)** 馬　**(e)** 綿羊

(f) 公雞　**(g)** 母雞　**(h)** 小雞　**(i)** 鵝　**(j)** 鴨子

⭐4. 你知道下面的蔬菜用英語怎麼説嗎？試説説看。

(a) 紅蘿蔔　**(b)** 豌豆　**(c)** 青瓜　**(d)** 南瓜　**(e)** 馬鈴薯

DICTIONARY 詞典

（英、粵、普發聲）

A

animal　動物

apricots　杏仁

asparagus　蘆筍

B

basket　籃子

bean　豆

beautiful　美麗

bedrooms　睡牀

behind　後面

bull　公牛

C

cabbage　椰菜

calf　小牛

carrot　紅蘿蔔

cat　貓

cauliflower　椰菜花

celery　西芹

chemicals　化學品

chick　小雞

clean　清潔

cock　公雞

corn　粟米（普：玉米）

countryside　郊外

courtyard　庭院

cow　母牛

cowshed　牛棚

crowing　啼叫

cucumber　青瓜

cultivated　耕種的

D

daisies　雛菊

delicious　美味

detective　偵探

dog　狗

25

donkey　驢子

drinks　喝

drive　駕駛

duck　鴨子

E

eggplant　茄子

eggs　蛋

F

farm　農場

farmhouse　農舍

feed　餵飼

feedstuff　飼料

field　田地

flower　花

forget　忘記

fresh　新鮮

G

garlic　蒜頭

goat　山羊

goose　鵝

grass　草

green bean　青豆

greenhouse　溫室

groom　照料

grow　生長

H

happened　發生

happy　快樂

hay　乾草

hayloft　乾草棚

healthy　健康的

hen　母雞

hen house　雞舍

herbivores　食草動物

hoe　鋤頭

home　家

horse　馬

how　怎樣

J

jealous　妒忌

L

lamb　小羊

lay eggs　下蛋

lettuce　生菜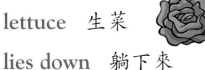

lies down　躺下來

M

middle　中間

miss　想念

mystery　神秘

N

naturally　自然地

O

of course　當然

onion　洋蔥

orchard　果園

organic vegetables　有機蔬菜

P

pea　豌豆

peacock　孔雀

picks　摘

pig　豬

pigeon　鴿子

plants　植物

plate　碟子

porch　門廊

potato　馬鈴薯

proud　自豪

pumpkin　南瓜

R

rabbit　兔子

rabbit warren　養兔場

radish　小蘿蔔

runs away　逃跑

S

sad　傷心

sheep　綿羊

sheep fold　羊圈

soil　泥土

solving　解決

sow　播種

spreads　展開

straw　稻草

strawberries　士多啤梨
　　（普：草莓）

sweet pepper　甜椒

T

tail　尾巴

tomato　番茄

tractor　拖拉機

turkey　火雞

turtle-dove　斑鳩

U

understand　明白

unusual　不尋常

upstairs　樓上

used　使用

V

vegetable garden　菜田

W

water　水 / 澆水

weather vane　風向計

well　井

what　什麼

when　什麼時候

where　哪裏

who　誰

why　為什麼

看在一千塊莫澤雷勒乳酪的份上，你學得開心嗎？很開心，對不對？好極了！跟你一起跳舞唱歌我也很開心！我等着你下次繼續跟班哲文和潘朵拉一起玩一起學英語呀。現在要說再見了，當然是用英語說啦！

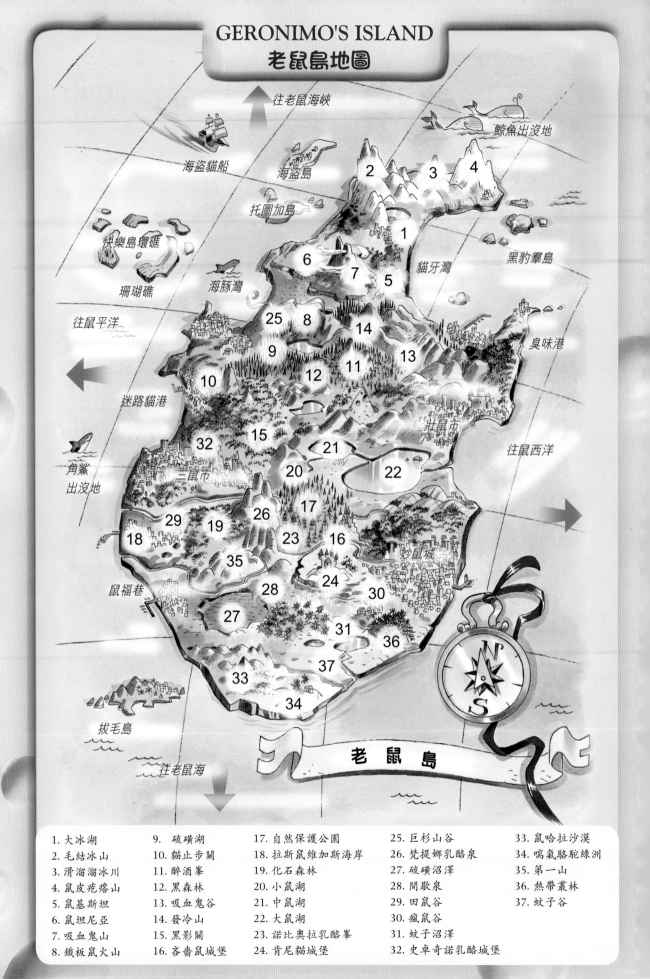

GERONIMO'S ISLAND
老鼠島地圖

往老鼠海峽

鯨魚出沒地

海盜貓船

海盜島

托圖加島

快樂島環礁

珊瑚礁

海豚灣

往鼠平洋

貓牙灣

黑豹羣島

臭味港

角鯊
出沒地

迷路貓港

壯鼠市

往鼠西洋

三鼠市

妙鼠城

鼠福巷

老鼠島

拔毛島

往老鼠海

Geronimo Stilton

EXERCISE BOOK
練習冊

想知道自己對 LET'S GO TO THE FARM! 掌握了多少，
趕快打開後面的練習完成它吧！

ENGLISH!

16 **LET'S GO TO THE FARM!** 到農場去！

GRANDMA ROSA'S FARM
羅莎婆婆的農場

★ 看看羅莎婆婆的農場，農場裏有些什麼？選出代表答案的英文
字母填在空格內。

A. sheep fold   B. cowshed   C. hay

D. orchard   E. vegetable garden

F. weather vane   G. hen house

H. well   I. courtyard

FARM ANIMALS
農場裏的動物

★ 農場裏有很多不同的動物，你都認識嗎？從下面選出適當的字詞填在橫線上，然後給圖畫填上顏色。

cat	goat	horse	donkey
bull	rabbit	sheep	calf
dog	lamb	pig	cow

1.  _____

2.  _____

3.  _____

4.  _____

5.  _____

6.  _____

7.  _____

8.  _____

9.  _____

10.  _____

11.  _____

12.  _____

POULTRY 家禽

⭐ 農場裏有很多不同的家禽，你都認識嗎？從下面選出適當的字詞填在橫線上，然後給圖畫填上顏色。

peacock	duck	chick	cock
turkey	hen	pigeon	goose

1.  _____

2.  _____

3.  _____

4.  _____

5.  _____

6.  _____

7.  _____

8.  _____

WHERE? WHAT? WHO? WHEN? WHY?
在哪裏？什麼？誰？ 什麼時候？為什麼？

⭐ 他們在說什麼？從下面選出適當的字詞填在橫線上，完成句子。

> **Why　　Where　　What　　Who　　When**

1. _____ eats corn?

2. _____ do cows eat?

3. _____ are you going to cut the grass?

_____ is the hay stored?

4.

5. _____ is the grass left to dry?

4

IN THE VEGETABLE GARDEN 在菜田裏

⭐ 菜田裏種了很多蔬菜。把蔬菜和相配的英文名稱用線連起來。

1. •　　　• A. carrot

2. •　　　• B. bean

3. •　　　• C. cabbage

4.  •　　　• D. cauliflower

5.  •　　　• E. eggplant

6.  •　　　• F. potato

7.  •　　　• G. pea

8.  •　　　• H. green bean

VEGETABLES 蔬菜

⭐ 根據圖畫，圈出正確的答案。

1.  4 (tomato / tomatoes)

2.  3 (onion / onions)

3.  2 (radish / radishes)

4.  5 (asparagus / asparaguses)

5.  6 (cucumber / cucumbers)

6. 1 (eggplant / eggplants)

POTTERING 耕種

⭐ 他們正在做什麼？從下面選出代表答案的英文字母填在空格內。

A. Benjamin picks strawberries.
B. Geronimo waters the salad plants.
C. In each hole, Pandora puts a plant.
D. Tea picks apples from the apple tree.
E. Rododendro makes holes in the ground.
F. Grandma Rosa shells the peas.

1.

2.

3.

4.

5.

6.

ANSWERS 答案

TEST　　小測驗

1. (a) field　　(b) vegetable garden　　(c) orchard　　(d) hay　　(e) greenhouse　　(f) courtyard
2. (a) The <u>vegetable garden</u> is <u>down</u> <u>there</u>.　　(b) May we <u>go</u> <u>up</u> <u>there</u>?
　　(c) <u>Who</u> eats corn?　　(d) <u>What</u> do <u>cows</u> eat?
3. (a) cow　(b) bull　(c) rabbit　(d) horse　(e) sheep　(f) cock　(g) hen　(h) chick　(i) goose　(j) duck
4. (a) carrot　　(b) pea　　(c) cucumber　　(d) pumpkin　　(e) potato

EXERCISE BOOK　　練習冊

P.1

P.2

1. cow　　2. horse　　3. bull　　4. rabbit　　5. calf　　6. pig
7. goat　　8. donkey　　9. sheep　　10. cat　　11. lamb　　12. dog

P.3

1. cock　　2. duck　　3. hen　　4. pigeon　　5. chick　　6. peacock　　7. goose　　8. turkey

P.4

1. Who　　2. What　　3. When　　4. Where　　5. Why

P.5

1. F　　2. G　　3. B　　4. H　　5. A　　6. C　　7. D　　8. E

P.6

1. tomatoes　　2. onions　　3. radishes　　4. asparaguses　　5. cucumbers　　6. eggplant

P.7

1. A　　2. D　　3. E　　4. C　　5. F　　6. B